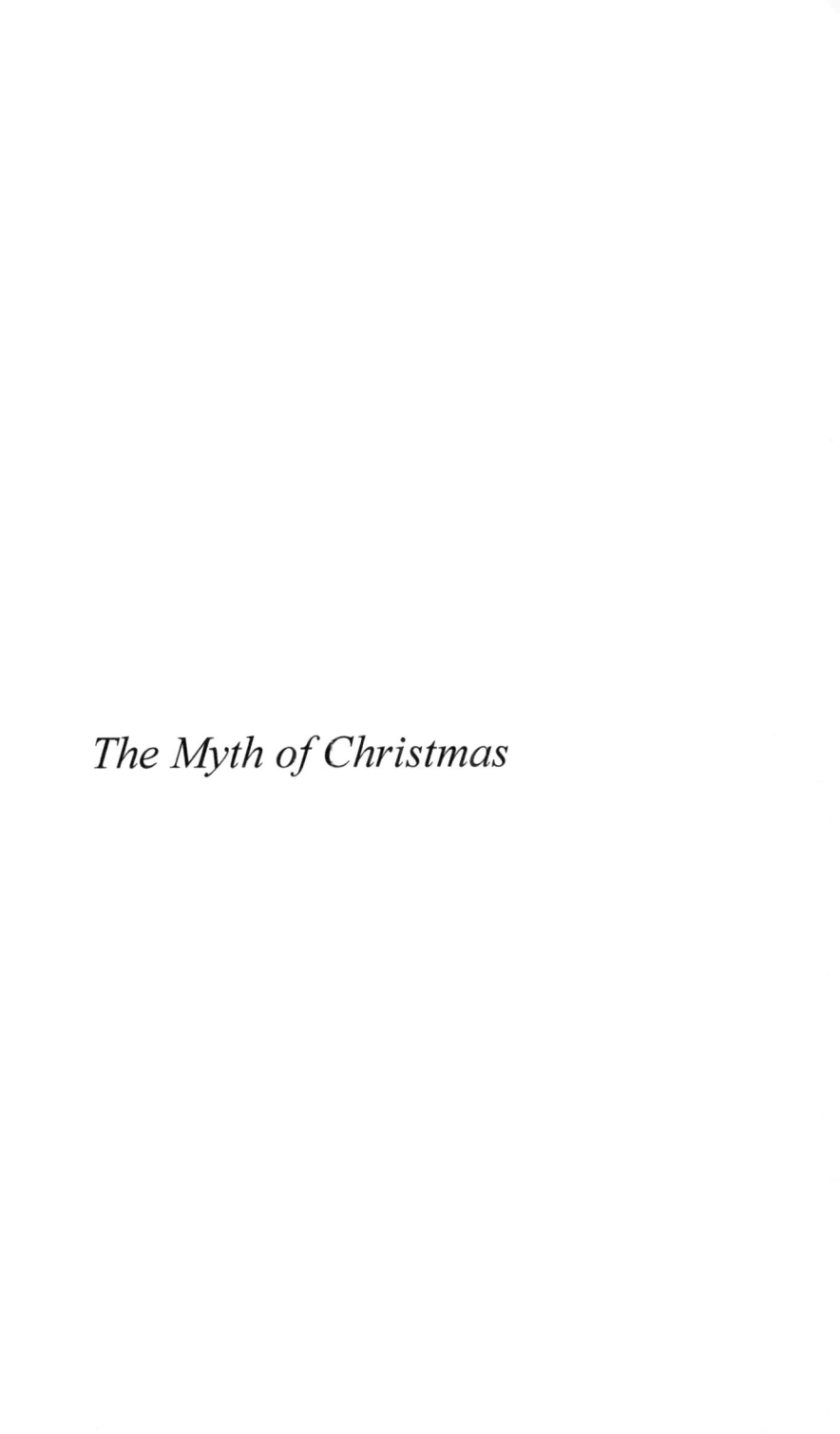

The Myth of Christmas

Murielle Lucie Clément

The Myth of Christmas

MLC

By the author :

Crime à l'université
Lettres de Sibérie
Comment devenir proustien sans lire Proust
La fabuleuse histoire d'Amsterdam et des Pays-Bas

Editions MLC
Le Montet – 36340 Cluis

© MLC 2015
ISBN : 978-2374320168
November 2015

To my friends

Content

Prologue

I was left with a pressing need to write this collection of personal accounts about Christmas after having directed an opera seminar for prisoners at the Hauts de Seine Prison.

We had worked for a week on Bizet's *Carmen* and the presentation of our efforts took place on the afternoon of December 24th. When the time came to say goodbye, I felt my heart sink. Not only was having to leave human beings behind bars and gates painful, so was the idea of putting up with the futile efforts of spending Christmas Eve with complete strangers. Despite the warmth and understanding coming from the guests, I felt closer to those with whom I had just shared so many emotions and such music. To add to the feeling of sorrow, the television news told the story of an airplane hijacking and Christmas night being ravaged by a destructive storm.

The return to my Amsterdam apartment was burdened with an invasive sadness, filled with the weighty memories of Christmases past. It was then that the black chasm of creation suddenly engulfed me and after having unplugged the telephone and confined myself in my bedroom, I allowed myself to be absorbed by the writing which would become *13 days of Christmas.* I outlined twelve accounts. They would come into being in less than two weeks, during which I wrote without respite, sleeping from time to time for an hour or two and taking up my pen upon awakening.

After having finished, I counted thirteen stories. If only someone would spare me from having to explain how that had happened! I wouldn't be able to say!!

Each carries within it the kernel of truth necessary to all expression. Products of the meandering pathways of memory, they are an homage to the generosity of those whom I have had the honor to cross on the road of Life; a testimony to their struggle for existence. Success? Failure? Would that it not have been in vain!

As soon as the collection was finished, the strength of the accounts seemed obvious. A few friends encouraged me to seek an editor. Why translate the manuscript into five languages? To make of it one book which can be read simultaneously all over the world! In the 21st century Europe is forming and we are going to have to communicate with one another if we are to avoid the global catastrophe which threatens us if we neglect to do so. For this, language is indispensable to us.

This collection is far from being the ultimate solution to the world's problems, but it is a stone for the foundation of the bridge, which we should throw over the divide separating us from one another. Let us try to remember that Christmas should be a festival of sharing.

Murielle Lucie Clément

Ave Maria

"Amen," echoes the congregation toward the priests, each dressed in an ivory chasuble draped over a crimson underskirt. Sitting in a neat line of straw chairs, their polished shoes placed together flat on the ground, their hands immobile on their knees, backs straight, chins freshly shaved, bright-eyed, hair combed, barely breathing, their gaze does not leave the eyes of the archbishop who has come to celebrate Christmas Mass.

"Dominus Sanctus," recites the archbishop in his deep voice.

"Amen," they respond in one attentive chorus.

Innumerable, exuberant candles spread a soft light, which caresses the frescos hidden in the shadows of the innermost recesses of the church. The deteriorated reds and blues jump and flutter in the raised billowing sleeves of tunics, wide like frigate sails from which gracefully plump feet with slender toes impishly emerge. Illuminated with mysterious smiles, framed by hair or an abundant disarray of ribbons, the faces of the young display a languorous expression full of commiseration. "Amen," the delicately carmine-rimmed lips seem to murmur. The gilding, brilliantly shimmering in the half-light, gives the impression of a world of abundance and gaiety.

"Ave Maria." An angel's voice comes to life. Pure, it soars toward the arched ceiling, tenderly coiling itself around the squat pillars;

gentle, it embeds itself in the censers, rebounds bewitchingly off the cold marble.

"Gratia plena." Bead by bead it says the rosary in mystical syllables. Beneath the vaulted ceiling where a sacred silence reigns, the petals of the lustres clink together imperceptibly, elegantly accompanying the voice with their crystalline notes.

"Dominus Tecum," warbles the virginal soloist. The timbre of her voice easily performs the permutations of the vowels, each polished with love and precision. The acoustics reverberate from vault to vault until reaching the apsidal chapels.

"Benedicta tu." Around her, the chorus attacks the harmony in full voice while in the central nave the faithful chant in a barely audible whisper.

"In mulieribus," murmurs the children's choir, quivering in the transept. Their leader had endlessly made them rehearse "Cantabile", circling his arms in tempo. "Cantabile" their bewitching voices ring out, tinkling like a stream over moss in the forest depths. The fluidity of their voices cascades in ephemeral roulades, flooding the edifice with a divine light which flows in whispering caresses over the base of the sculpted arches.

"Et benedictus fructus," the ardently devoted assembly breaks into song, their voices trembling with meticulous precision. The thrum of their voices makes its way toward the crucifix with devoted piety.

In the twilight, irradiated with a diaphanous glow, sits the cross, shining in refringent brilliance, reflecting a proliferation of glistening rays in diffuse shimmers. His head resting on his shoulder, his bloodied palms stretched far, far from his chest – at the extremities of his extended arms, He can barely withstand his mutilated body, wrapped in a silver loincloth. The Savior crosses his feet, fastened with a cord knotted around the ankles. His curved forehead crowned with diamond thorns, He cries tears of vermilion, emerald, and blood.

"Ventris tui." The throats warble their last trills, projecting a final appeal to the dawn approaching through the stained-glass windows. Feathers ruffled, a drowsy turtledove emphasizes the all-encompassing silence with a discreet snort. The last notes dissipate imperceptibly in a fog of incense. Amen.

The scraping of chairs pushed with nonchalance against the tiles bring the faithful back to earth. Their furtive soles polish the large black and white chessboard, bringing them directly toward the wide-open entryway. Their silhouettes bustle about in enchanting shadows on a bright azure background created by the meeting of sky and sea. Half-blinded by the sudden brightness, they linger on the church square in their holiday finery. Coiffured in stiffly starched turbans, the women triumphantly display their gleaming opaline ivory dresses, whose multitudinous flounced skirts slash at their calves and whose frills stir the desire of the men, also dressed in white. Sprays of sweet-smelling pale yellow lilies are piled into overburdened arms, mingling their fragrance with the crowns of braided roses. Laughter mixing, fingers interlacing, eyes enticing, they promise to meet again after the ceremony. A shiver runs through the crowd. The bishop and the soloist exit the church. They converse in low voices. They turn to face one another, hesitate, and advance a few more steps. For a moment, they both stand still, blinking their eyes as they meet the light once again. Then it is the Virgin's turn to greet the day. Hoisted onto a wooden dais carried on the arms of men, clothed in her loveliest attire, she dominates the crowd as they reverently make the sign of the cross. The persistent drums beat a deafening rhythm. Subdued, the procession sets off smoothly, taking the road to Pelourino. Accompanied by a samba, Maria makes the tour of the old quarter. Those who do not follow her throw an offering of flowers as she passes, others throw her kisses; all pay respectful homage.

The sun has risen higher in the sky and the heat has engulfed the stones, trembling in unison with the huge drum. A triangle unflaggingly strikes the powerful beats while drumsticks frenetically pound the tight drum skins. High heels rhythmically pound the cobblestones, rounded like the bald heads of newborn infants. The women, weighed down by the hazy humidity, mop their brows while laughing, cursing the waxed polish of their new shoes. One of them dares to be the first to liberate herself from the constraint, and she is soon followed by her sisters who prefer bare feet to the festive decorum. Sweat forms beads on all foreheads, makes rings under the arms. Just a little further and a satisfied Maria will rejoin the coolness of her tabernacle for a year. The parade pushes, clutching, attacks the coast, and in a halting convulsion arranges itself on the steps leading to the basilica. Having completed the unavoidable chore, they surge with relief into the gaping nave, sprawling shamelessly on the wicker chairs. Some fan themselves with a missal, others pinch their clothes above their arms, raising the cloth from their skin between thumb and forefinger, squirming to get a little air. They breathe noisily, stimulated by the accomplished task.

Maria, bedecked with her necklaces, rests on her gilded pedestal. The bells peal out, pulled forcefully by volunteers hanging onto the ropes. Calmly, in small groups, the faithful make merry, heading off to the beach or toward the center of town, many toward Mercado Modelo, the port where restaurants invite them. There they will shell vermilion crabs with giant legs, savor pigs' feet with brown beans and saffron pork rinds served with rice, smack their lips at beef fricassee with manioc. A few couples form. They have other appetites.

White Christmas

The milky white expanse sparkles under a cloudless sky, evening out any rough patches in the countryside, enrobing them in a soft cottony padding with bluish sparks, pink in places. The trunks of young silver birches, those which were left standing for the next cut, disappear from view, merge into their surroundings. The old trees, sawed into pieces and piled in staggered rows, are unsullied mounds to the top of which only magpies and crows venture.

His back turned to the forest, Micha stands absorbing this winter vision, this savage purity capable of inspiring grandiloquent speeches, to the point of bursting. The still air surrounds him like a bubble of liquid glass which shifts itself according to his movements, crystal through which the far-off line of the horizon appears, there where from time to time the vague silhouette of a herd of white deer is outlined.

"Over there, over there," Micha sings to himself.

To his right, unaware of his presence, a silver fox springs up unexpectedly. He dashes into a tunnel in the snow, his bushy tail wagging in the wind. Under his breath, Micha wishes him good hunting. He knows that times are hard for all beings of the forest.

After having meticulously scrutinized the sky, he is certain that the subsided storm will not return, at least not for a few days. The temperature will drop considerably, however. His breathing will prick at his lungs like needles, he will feel his eyes grate at his eyelids, not a single unnecessary word will pass his lips. He will move parsimoniously, economically, scrupulously gauging his expended effort, every ill-considered gesture containing the threat of death. Micha sighs. Pulling his log-laden sleigh behind him, he continues walking. The mauve snow reflects the orange rays from the sun which will not set. Along the way, he discovers a few traps and jams their frozen capture into the bottom of his pouch.

Hundreds, perhaps thousands, squelch through the icy mud before the barracks, transforming the ground into a mucky out-of-season thaw. Not a murmur, not a word escapes from the tattered crowd. Waiting patiently and silently, the bodies with pallid faces, eyes bulging with apprehension, strain their ears to pick up the silence. Sustained by their disciplined hope for a hypothetical ration, they have arranged themselves into a thick, winding line which makes no progress. When the door of the barracks finally opens, a light rustle waves through the skeletal men and women. Seeing the captain instills in them a fleeting, uncontrollable shudder. Of fear or of hope? None could say with certainty.

His face wedged between his collar and wolfskin cap, his eyes stare at the human mass without seeing it. A contemptuous grin issuing from the corner of his mouth, his golden incisors bite out the fateful message, "No provisions! Not today, not tomorrow!" The words fly through the crowd, brushing past their malnourished bodies. The tension which had reached its height with the appearance of the officer escapes from the crowd. A long sigh of discouragement strips the people of any emotion. A burst balloon. They will fast for Christmas.

Meanwhile, at the far end of the camp, in a corner sheltered from wind and from watchful eyes, Micha blows onto a fire. Above the embers reddened by the flames, impaled on a small steel spit, a skinned rat cooks slowly.

The Christmas Tree

Taking cover behind the clouds, the gloomy weather lies in wait for an indication to emerge. It watches the light breeze intently, ready to attack it with a rain shower as soon as it dies down. Protected behind the living room's large picture window, Bernadette, bustling about near the hearth, impatiently awaits her youngest son Sylvain. Today, with his new girlfriend, he will come share Christmas dinner. She would have preferred him to be there on Christmas Eve, to have him close to her, but she understood that the only way not to alienate herself from him completely was to let him be free. Yesterday, for the first time since her sons were born, she had had to content herself with the company of her eldest. Although she had not let it show, the separation weighed upon her. All the more so because she is always obliged to put on a bold front in the face of her daughter-in-law, a Pole, who has obviously set her heart on Olivier to settle her visa problems. It is clear that if Aliona's papers had been in order, there would have been no marriage. No mother-in-law for Olivier, either. At least not immediately, not officially, and Bernadette could have avoided keeping company with that surly, forbidding woman with whom she cannot exchange three words.

In any case, Aliona's mother is impossible. Always disapproving of her daughter, demoralizing her, and the worst, which

Bernadette really cannot stand, endlessly making disagreeable remarks regarding Olivier. Remarks which, incidentally, Aliona hastens to report to her in full and without fail. Of course, it is true that Olivier is not exactly well organized; he's a jazz musician. For artists, life can be difficult. However, she believes in his talent; since he was a very little boy, she always supported him. She is certain that one of these days he will make a name for himself and will be very capable of standing on his own two feet. Pavla, Aliona's mother, reproaches him for staying in bed all morning. Bernadette has really tried, with the aid of Aliona, who has proven herself to be an indispensable translator, to explain to her that he has always been like that. Even as a baby he would sleep until noon, not getting into action until the end of the afternoon.

According to Pavla he suffered from a lack of discipline; that a person's nature should give in to willpower as their character is formed. To Bernadette it's clear: Pavla's theory is based on her country's old ways of thinking. In spite of that, not speaking a word of Polish and Pavla only able to speak a bit of French, they have been able to avoid extended discussions on the subject up until this point.

She lays the kindling and the logs in a carefully designed alternation. Normally, Sébastien lights the fireplace, but for the moment he has gone to pick up his mother, who will also participate in the feast. It's not as though Bernadette likes the old woman, but as it's expected that she invite her every once in a while, it might as well be this evening. That way she will be relieved of one familial duty.

Bernadette smiles while thinking of her husband. She likes the way he has of telling her that she has set about doing something the wrong way, that the flames will never spread if the logs are placed like that. Over the course of twenty years of marriage, their relationship has been solidly constructed. Rites lacking in disloyalty have built up between them, and gentle replies form the stable foundation of their happiness. Walking around the room, she blocks from her view the young pine tree at the end of the table, a gift from Aliona's mother. To refuse the present would have been against the rules of politeness, not to mention those of hospitality. However, she felt that the woman had cunningly interfered in her personal life, going to the extent of bringing a Christmas tree from Poland! What a ridiculous symbol of her joining their family! Full of seething rage, Bernadette had bought a tree three meters tall. Never mind that they had had to saw off the top! It is she who is mistress of this house. That Pavla should call Olivier "my son" will never change that!

She had managed to convince the boys to decorate the tree, a fact which she had astutely slipped into the conversation several times at dinner. Pavla had had a hard time responding to that, especially since she could not follow the discussion if Aliona inadvertently failed in her duty as interpreter.

Bernadette would have liked her sons to remain small, or to have them grow up without bringing her daughters- and mothers-in-law. They would have decorated her tree, just one. They would have taken part in Christmas Eve with her friends rather than passing it God knows where. But now they're either gone for the holidays, confronting her with the loneliness which is the lot of old couples, or they come accompanied by awful strangers who she is required to work into her schedule.

A gust of wind blows into the room when Sylvain and Sabrina arrive. Bernadette embraces them warmly, pressing them to her heart like prisoners of war returned from the enemy camp. Sabrina has made no effort whatsoever in her appearance. Her black trousers, which she wears to high school, are worn through at the knees. She wears a shapeless sweater of an uncertain color and smeared makeup around eyes half hidden by aggressive forelocks, giving a dubious impression. But what upsets Bernadette the most are her brown, muddy combat boots placed proudly and distinctly on the flowered carpet, denoting a conscious provocation and lack of elegance. She feels as though her toes are being crushed by the young girl's soles.

She proposes an aperitif in order to choke back the disapproving remark which is working its way up to her lips. She offers them the choice between a blackberry kir and champagne, brings glasses and appetizers. Cheerful, a good actress, she sits down after having served the new arrivals. She accepts the situation, avoids looking at the shoes.

"Your tree is awful. That's no way to decorate a Christmas tree! You have balls of all different colors, and your garlands are hanging vertically. At our house we use only white garlands circled *around* the tree and a few balls of one and the same shade. And you don't even have electric lights! It's really pathetic."

Bernadette is entirely too flabbergasted to be able to say anything other than a weak "Ah!" Encouraged by the dumbfounded silence of her audience, Sabrina continues in a pertinent tone,

"And your garlands are really ugly, all tattered. Look at those things there, there in the corner, what are those? Cotton? Snowmen? They're old, shabby, and faded. No one uses those things anymore. Furthermore, you have two trees. One would think you had just dumped the box of decorations over the thing, as if it were a garbage can. They've been decorated without love."

Before Bernadette can voice the sharp objection rising up within her and impolitely rebuff the young girl, putting her severely in her place, Sébastien makes an entrance which could not be better timed. Diplomatically, he steers his mother before him, pushing her gently into the living room. Never had Bernadette been so happy to see her mother-in-law.

The Red Fort

Georges raises his head. High in the sky, raptors circle above the city, surveying the comings and goings in the thoroughfares, seeking the tiniest indication of an easy prey, a possible means of sustenance. Their presence gives concrete expression to the vague threat which weighs each of his steps.

Upon arriving at the airport, all his worldliness, everything he thought he knew, had been swept away by the comparative reality of the moment. Even the bus rocking about on the overheated tar pierced through his comportment. He had been told it was a bus, but the vehicle was not what he had expected. He had never seen anything like it. It had four wheels and a chassis, a windshield, probably a motor to propel it forward, but the analogy ended there.

"Welcome to Delhi, International Arrivals"

"Welcome to Delhi," written in welcoming capital letters, contrasted astonishingly with the second part of the announcement, forming a flagrant disparity.

"International Arrivals." So often he had read the same in the farthest corners of Europe, but the context here was unrecognizable! The corrugated iron roofs inflicted the surprise of an enlightening anachronism upon him, inadvertently placed in the ochre and yellowish dust. Two or three hours had passed since the moment he had entered the building and the moment he left it. However, no unusual formality had occurred. They had asked him to produce his passport and stamped it two or three times after he had made a statement that he had nothing to declare. The process was in every sense similar to Charles de Gaulle, Leonardo da Vinci or Heathrow. Only the slowness of the procedure had been surprising. His first confrontation with the tempo governing the city had taken place.

Back in the free world, he experienced an indescribable and disconcerting sensation; an unsatisfied curiosity possessed him. December. He had left the ice and snow, the furs and the boots behind him. Sun, short sleeves, trees in bloom, and sun tanning greeted him, unusual visions which transported him into the fleeting timelessness of constant climatologic difference. Whether he should choose a taxi or a rickshaw to reach his destination, he would not be able to avoid the scraggy dogs on the lookout for stinking remains, and above all he would have to give out tips and alms. The overwhelming dilemma of cultural difference assailed him. The beggars were even present at meetings. The women were draped in dust-covered saris which outlined their curves in modest veils, the men dressed in ancestral rags which Georges could not discern as being shorts or skirts. But he could not ignore the fact that without exception, they all reached out their hands for an alm which he was still incapable of giving them, so much was he restricted by the shackles of his Parisian habits. In a hurry, always in a hurry, too much time lost at customs! Faster, faster! Escape into a car, toss out the name of a street, close himself off into his thoughts. He had, however, had the time to notice the scarlet-flowered hedges. That had been three days ago. An eternity.

He had wandered about all morning and now let himself be driven in a rickshaw towards Lal Qila, the Red Fortress. Yesterday afternoon, he had visited Gandhi's tomb, dazzled by the black polished marble covered in orange and yellow French marigolds. Most of the visitors bore large garlands of real flowers around their necks, which streaked their immaculately pressed and starched white cotton dress like flashes of lightning. The men punctuated their discussions with large gestures, walked around the mausoleum in groups, conversed about quotations on the stock exchange. Full of laughter, young girls picnicked, opened baskets, claimed their favorite foods, went into raptures over the heaps of provisions, wrapped in cloths of various colors.

The crimson pink walls of the fortress, erected at the end of the avenue, display the appropriateness of its name. The driver drops Georges off at the main entrance after weaving a slalom course between the visitors and peanut vendors. He glimpses entire families seated at the foot of the ramparts. The tarmac is their home, a piece of blanket serving as furniture. Their entire lives take place on these few square meters, uniting several generations, the warm air their only possession. Here, to be homeless means to be born, to live, and to die in the street. On the sidewalk, you cook, you sleep, and you fornicate. All of the major and minor daily happenings occur in plain view, where anyone can see. Intimacy takes place on another plane, as does respect for human life.

It has been ages since the fort contained treasure, since its wonders had disappeared in repeated pillages by bands of thieves, successive governments, and British colonists. Nonetheless, among the darkened ruins, Georges can still imagine the ancient splendor showing through the remnants, announcing their former grandeur. He allows himself to be carried away by the atmosphere created by these souvenirs of wealth, mitigated by the view of the present misery. He buys a bouquet of peacock feathers, the shimmering of which bring to mind the jewels of the vanished maharajahs. Having exited the castle compound, he strolls in the old quarter.

The closer he gets to Jama Mashid, the grand mosque, the less breathable the air becomes. His nostrils tortured by the acrid odors of goat, urine, and defecation, obsessed with the spectacle of the dying, he continues. He strides over the yellow sand path and the bodies who have come to blend into nothingness.

A man, grounded wreckage on the banks of life, lies naked. He groans. A sickening rumbling raises his abdomen in spasmodic convulsions, his lips tense in pain, his eyes roll back under his closed eyelids, lowered in an ultimate sense of modesty. He dies. His putrid breath invites death's clutches. Georges cannot turn his eyes from the man who no longer sees him despite the sun flooding his face where sweat will never again break out.

Drowned in the sapphire sky, incandescent beams freeze the scene with their haughty, imperious rays. Staring straight ahead, the indifferent crowd nonchalantly brushes past the deceased. A few curious onlookers bustle about further ahead, studying a dying man stretched out in the scraggy shade of a eucalyptus tree. Georges emerges from his stupor. Nothing around him brings the day of the Nativity to mind.

Flight 7.45

Jean-Claude takes off his overcoat and stuffs it in the baggage compartment above his seat. He sits down, buckles his seatbelt, and unfolds his newspaper. He can finally relax. He has won the race against the clock and will be spending Christmas Eve with his family. Ahead of him lie four days of rest which he has promised to dedicate entirely to Hélène and the children. A miniature tree, spotted with tiny, incandescent bronzed apples, reminds him that it is Christmas. Wrapped in a mink coat, a large blonde woman bursts into the central aisle. Her high-pitched voice proclaims disapproval, to the attention of no one. Her swollen hands twirl with illustrative agility, punctuating her babbling with demented gestures, highlighted by flashes from her rings. The flight attendant has seen plenty of her type before and would not get upset for so little. Impassive, a friendly smile plastered on her charming face, she listens patiently. Above all, never contradict the passengers. Jean-Claude cannot stop himself from scrutinizing her face, which he thinks he recognizes.

Her eyes, overloaded with fake eyelashes thickened with mascara and enlarged by generously applied makeup in an Egyptian style, stretch back to her temples. Her hair has been pulled back and gathered at the nape of her neck in a heavy chignon which seems to start at her forehead. A large tortoiseshell comb flecked with diamonds betrays her Andalousian origins. Her cheeks jut out under the rouge. Her exaggeratedly articulating purple lips solemnly and steadfastly massage her teeth.

"But Miss, there must be some mistake! I don't smoke."

The young woman repeats without the slightest trace of irritation that, although there are ashtrays provided, the woman's seat is located in the non-smoking section.

"Besides, this gentleman is the only other passenger," she says, indicating Jean-Claude with a friendly nod of the head.

Reassured, after an affirmative sign towards an imaginary entourage the latecomer consents to part with her fur, helped by the still smiling young woman.

The reason for the commotion remains unclear to Jean-Claude, who delves back into his article. As usual, at the time of take-off his mind goes blank and he feels a weight in the pit of his stomach. The imposing number of flights to his credit change nothing.

The engines burst into life, thrumming with a high-pitched intensity audible even in the cabin. The runway passes more quickly under the wing, his back presses more heavily against his seat, he stops reading to feel the machine lift at the moment his thighs slacken. The wheels leave the ground. The ascent of the aircraft begins. He knows that he will not be able to relax until they reach cruising altitude. Until then, the sort of feverish stupor he suffers will not leave him.

A sudden relaxation running through his muscles tells him that they have reached the required altitude. Instinctively he goes back to reading, seeking the thread of his story amongst the lines of printed characters. He accepts a graciously offered glass of champagne, but politely refuses the plate of snacks which are supposed to be tempting. He doesn't like caviar. Whether it be red or black, he cannot stand the taste of granulated fish.

The prattle of the blonde woman reaches him as background noise in the distance. He feels more than he sees the steward fold up his newspaper and cover his legs with a light blanket.

He is awoken by yelling. Before him, a man he has never seen before is brandishing a gun, motioning him to stand up. He does so with caution. The stranger pats him, runs his hand over his seat, and pushes him violently back down. The platinum passenger has disappeared. A second man comes out of the cabin leading to the cockpit. Only when he looks a few rows further does he catch sight of the slumped body of his neighbor. Ringlets of hair escape from her chignon with the jerking movements of her head, signifying that the irreversible has not yet occurred.

The newly arrived man exchanges words with the man who just frisked him in a staccato language with guttural accents, the sense of which escapes him. A third associate pulls back the curtain, bursting in before him. He has come from coach. How many of them are there? They stand in a whispering huddle outside of his field of vision. He would prefer to close his eyes, but in spite of everything he keeps them open.

Straining his ears, he absorbs snatches of incomprehensible sentences. Is it a good or a bad sign that he is still in the same seat? He tries to analyze the situation, but lacks references. He curses himself for never having read an official hijacking report. Because the evidence speaks for itself: they are the victims of a group of terrorists or gangsters. Surreptitiously, he looks at his watch. They should have started their descent into Charles de Gaulle half an hour ago. He has no idea where they are. It's not a watch he needs but a compass. The view of perfect clouds amongst rays of sun does not help him determine their latitude. At the very most he knows that they are still too high up to announce an approaching landing. From the position of the sun, he deduces that they have not changed direction. The aircraft begins a turn to the left without slowing down, causing the cabin to vibrate strongly. Is a different pilot at the controls? The door at the end of the cabin opens. Wrists tied behind their backs, pushed with the nose of a gun, the hostess and the steward walk through the rows of seats. At this moment, the fur lady decides to get up, which she does with difficulty. She emits a muffled grunt at seeing the weapon pointed at her and staggers toward the dark doorway. A command bellowed in English does not interrupt her progress. Clasping her hands, she continues toward the group at the other end of the cabin. With a gesture accentuating his rank, the man signals her to stand still.

Her jaws clenched, spattered with red spittle, her cheeks gray, streaked with black, she no longer sees him nor his mortal weapon.

She has gone beyond the limits of reason. Her spirit is roaming in a place where no words can reach her.

Jean-Claude cannot tear his eyes from the scene. His nostrils dilated, he breathes through his teeth, clamped so hard together they are about to break. The atrociousness of this scene, strange and familiar at the same time, unrolls before his eyes, leaving him powerless to change the slightest detail. In his head, the sound of a champagne cork popping and the animal cry of the blonde woman occurs simultaneously.

Her face deformed by the grimace of a fierce beast, she throws herself in one leap toward the round eye fixed upon her. The angry flame spits out a destructive kernel and the shot cuts her down headlong. The chignon comes apart, tumbling down heavily and silently onto her sagging shoulders. Time breaks down into little transparent bubbles which bounce around slowly in the interval of the death. They revolve in large circles, suffocating the silence in order to freeze the moment into a horrific instant. They gradually transform into a flower with modest pink petals, sprinkling the wrinkled alabaster forehead with crimson. They explode in fury at the sound of the fall and nimbly vanish into the cracks in eternity.

The hostess and the steward mutely step over the body and disappear into the cockpit. Jean-Claude realizes dumbly that he will never again hear the large woman whimper or howl. Her corpse sprawled out on the checkered cobalt carpet seems eloquent to him. The worst is staring him in the face.

The killer comes back alone and without saying a word puts the metal to Jean-Claude's temple. He remains motionless, allowing the inescapable reality of the moment to sink in. A purple apple falls from the tree and rolls to his feet, stopping at the edge of his shoe. Perplexed, he stares at it stupidly, squinting vacantly at its shining roundness, astonished by its variegated hue swelled with veins of old gold. Before the fire can warm him eternally, one luminous thought attaches itself pertinently to his consciousness. Discouraged, he dies. Yet another Christmas which he will not be able to spend with Hélène and the children.

December 24

I see their heads along the top of the privet hedge. My uncle leads the way in a soldierly manner while my aunt, the trooper, follows on his heels. For a moment the pillar of the doorway blocks them from my view. I widen my eyes so as to be able to see clearly the turning of the doorknob, solid proof of their arrival. Only strangers would ring the bell; family opens the door without formality. The door gets stuck halfway, then pushes back the layer of snow and opens wide. Framed in the doorway is the awaited couple. My Uncle Victor and my Aunt Lucette have finally arrived.

Ignoring my mother's cries to put on a coat before going outside, I run to greet them. They are my favorites. They never treat me as a child, they never say, "You've grown!" or "How's school?" They consider me their equal; we have real conversations. Snowflakes flutter in the cold night air, tickling my cheeks with their frozen kisses.

"Get back inside, you'll catch cold," says my uncle while hugging me.

I run my hand along my aunt's garnet-colored coat. It's soft, just like her.

"How's the food coming along?"

My aunt bursts into laughter after having kissed me on the forehead.

"You know you can count on Mom for that! She probably hasn't left the kitchen for a week!"

"So it'll be a real feast then!"

"You bet! But only after mass. This year it's decided. Everyone agrees. First church, then the banquet when we get back."

"In that case, we'll have more than enough time to build up an appetite!"

"Don't worry, there are hors d'œuvres."

"We're saved!"

"I thought I told you not to go out in your slippers!" scolds my mother half seriously, standing in the kitchen doorway. I retort that I put a shawl over my shoulders instead. Today is a holiday, and given that she never slaps me in front of her little sister, I can take advantage by getting on her nerves without risking any serious consequences.

I look at my uncle admiringly as he removes his overcoat, revealing his elegant bottle-green suit. I would so much have liked him to be my father! He's a real man. He has a carefully trimmed mustache which shadows his lip with an eternal smile. He has brilliantined curly black hair with no visible part and short sideburns ornamenting his cheeks. I am proud of him. He's always up to something exciting. Recently he bought two horses just for the pleasure of watching them frolic in a meadow. I like the way he drives his car and, above all, that he often takes me with him to the woods. There he shows me where the chanterelles and the morels hide, as well as the lilies of the valley in May. In summer he marks the tracks of the wild game he will hunt in the autumn. I like the spirited energy around him when he's hunting, to see his well-trained dogs respond to his slightest whistle.

I know that he only ever takes one piece of game at a time, and that often going hunting is only a pretext for him to go walking in the countryside. Without him telling me, I understood all that one day when I saw him smooth the feathers of a pheasant hen which one of his dogs had just brought him. Although it had been he who had killed it, he caressed the neck with love, arranging the bird's ruffled down before stuffing it into his gamebag. Another time, I saw both he and my aunt completely crushed when he had accidentally killed a female hare which was still lactating. They thought of the abandoned bunnies who they couldn't save because they didn't know where the burrow was located.

To me, my uncle is a real hero; straightforward, strong, and tenderhearted.

He's not like my father who, while a braggart, is afraid of a rifle. He refuses to hunt and criticizes the enjoyment of others. My mother was just barely able to convince him to begin fishing. I can understand why, it's less dangerous.

On the other hand, to give credit where credit is due, my father is a champion oyster opener and the end-of-the-year dinners give him a moment to shine. With a large navy-blue apron tied around his waist, he remains unbeatable. Not one of my uncles contests his superiority. Even Uncle Totor cannot keep up with his ability to pop the shells off of crustaceans. With a slight pressure on the blade inserted into a crevice only he has been able to discover, he separates the two halves without letting the oyster meat break. My mother flushes with pleasure at seeing her husband gain on the other participants. His plate fills with lighting speed. Not only is my dad the fastest, but he arranges his shellfish in a fan shape, mingling the *palourde* and *praire* clams with the *claire* and *Belon* oysters. After having added prawns, mussels, langoustines, and periwinkle, he proudly announces that his seafood platter is complete. My father is an artist.

While the men play at being master oyster-shellers for a day and the women exchange a few recipes while putting the finishing touches on dinner, the children are in charge of the table decoration. "The children" include my cousin Josiane, two years my elder (who insists that I must obey her because of this fact), her brother Gérard (called Ninou), my little sister (who is six years younger than me and with whom I have little in common because of the age difference), and myself.

My cousin Josiane has designated herself in charge of the project. She's jealous because I already made some place cards which open onto two pages. On one side is a drawing of Santa Claus and on the other, written in beautiful calligraphy letters in colored ink, the menu. On the face, I glued pine needles in the shape of a tree under the name of the guest. It's obvious that everyone will be thrilled with my creation.

To overcome her jealousy, Josiane has attempted to think up a staggeringly beautiful centerpiece, made by interlacing ribbons, pinecones, branches, and candles, twisting around the plates. The tablecloth is lost under the verdant disorder, which almost hides my place cards. Long ago the little ones, unguarded, abandoned us to empty a box of chocolates they opened without permission. Concentrated on our competition, we forgot to report their misdeed, however punishable, to the kitchen. They take advantage of this opportunity to stuff themselves with sweets, as their chocolate-smeared faces testify. They grow bold, going to the extent of offering us a piece, rendering us complicit in their gourmet larceny.

After having placed the menus in the glasses where they would be visible, I declare the decoration complete. Trying to outdo me, Josiane would have liked to change something about the placement of the foliage, but the adults return from the kitchen and enthusiastically praise our creation, reconciling us in a well-deserved shared success.

No one mentions midnight mass after the aperitifs and hors d'œuvres. The topic of discussion is more centered on sitting down to eat, which we do. A wind of disappointment blows through me. Yet again I will not get to see what this mass, discussed each year with such fervor, is like. The approach of my long hoped for revelation blends into the commotion of the conversation, deferred for at least another year. The only mass I have seen was my cousin's First Communion. She was the belle of the ball, with, I should add, at least a hundred other kids dressed in white. Nonetheless I would really have liked to be in her shoes on her day of glory. She received gifts from all who were invited, which were as extraordinary as they were unexpected. My mother, her godmother, gave her a gold watch, a gift which she had never given to me, her daughter. "That's because you're not having your Communion," she had said. And whose fault is that?

On the table the seafood platters have given over to the first courses. Standing on layers of mixed vegetables, hard-boiled eggs topped with mayonnaise-flecked tomato halves bring toadstools to mind, while tufts of curly parsley are "the spitting image" of a moss-covered ground and tomatoes cut to look like little baskets overflow with baby vegetables. On the large platters of meats, slices of sausage are arranged in petals, forming huge flowers with eyes of mortadella. Artichoke hearts are surrounded by fanned gherkins and triangles of brown bread piled in pyramids, decorating the four corners of the table. Next to them are placed honeycomb-shaped dishes of piping hot parsleyed *escargots*.

"We have to eat them right away or else they'll get cold."

We pass the round plates to everyone.

"You have to have white bread with *escargots*!"

"And white wine, right?"

A huge burst of laughter. The festivities have begun.

"Your *escargots* are good," comments my Uncle Guy.

The verdict has been passed. Guy, nicknamed Doll because of his blue eyes, is the reigning expert in the subject at hand. Two dishes must receive his approval for a meal to be successful: the *escargots* and the calf's head in vinaigrette. Mom says it's because he was poor as a boy and that these two dishes have always remained delicacies to him.

Every member of the family has their culinary specialty. For my Aunt Lulu, Lucette, it's sauerkraut. She lines the base of a casserole with pork rinds, heats it, and places a peeled Cox apple midway in the alternating layers of raw sauerkraut (not washed but rinsed in a colander) and meats.

My Aunt Julienne, the eldest of everyone, reigns at the head of the table. She is the queen of cassoulet, having been born in Castelnaudary, near Toulouse. So as not to be outdone, her husband, my Uncle José, has specialized in rabbit, wild rabbit of course, with chanterelles. Not just a few to embellish the sauce, but as vegetables, browned in the fat from smoked lean bacon.

My Aunt Suzon, Josiane and Gérard's mother, has a special touch for desserts and anything that is wrapped in puff pastry. It goes without saying that her meat pies are famous. I suspect that her husband excels in fruit brandies in order to succeed her in the presentation order of the courses. Cherries, blackberries, peaches, blackcurrants, grapes; he has tried them all more or less successfully, but it is the bigarreau cherries which have won the family's unanimous vote.

My Uncle Victor succeeds unparalleled in old-fashioned potted fowl; even my aunts envy his mastery of the skill. My mother is not very good at pastries, which I bitterly regret, but her meats, particularly her roasts, are always perfectly done, which prompted my father to dedicate himself to sautéed veal in white wine and potatoes. It's a recipe entirely of his own invention. But the list would not be complete if I forgot to mention my Uncle Charles's coq au vin with bacon and poached eggs.

With us, a family meal does not only include enjoying the dishes presented; we also evaluate each person's recipe, thus doubly enjoying the meal. Once the white sausages have been gobbled up and the vegetable platters have been cleared comes the moment for the turkey to make its entrance.

Surrounded by chestnuts, it sits imposingly upon its oval silver platter with golden handles. In our family, the poultry is cut on the table. No stolen morsels behind closed doors. The shears used especially for the job cut the crisp skin, the pink juices barely oozing from the damaged flesh.

"Perfectly done!" is the general judgment.

There follows a discussion about the different qualities of the stuffings used over the years and the question of whether we wouldn't do better, for a change, to have a goose next Christmas. The option is to be seriously considered, as a goose is after all fattier than a turkey. One thing is certain, we will never again serve young guineafowl, judged to be too dry. When all is said and done, the turkey will remain on the menu. It presents undeniable and considerable advantages, among others that of being "really Christmassy". An established expression, understood by each of us: "That's Christmassy" or "That's not Christmassy". This is the reason that every year, although we almost do not make it, we continue with a cheese platter after the *pièce de résistance*, followed by more or less exotic salads, and finish with a Yule Log, not to forget the ice cream. Nobody really likes the Yule Log, but it's Christmassy. We are inveterate mules and nothing will make us change, not even our sullen taste for this tradition.

A few hours later, the bird carcass and the haggard remains swimming the salad bowls are sent back to the kitchen and the coffeepot makes its appearance on the stained tablecloth. This is my favorite moment, the time for stories and songs, everyone wanting to do theirs first. Out of a kind of politeness they all act as if they need persuading, but no one would want to miss their moment in the spotlight. Even we kids have the right to step onto the stage, to have our moment of glory in the applause. All genres are allowed. We warble, shout, or hum according to our moods and our abilities. Then, every year one of us begins in a slightly more fragile voice to recite " 'Twas the Night Before Christmas", listened to reverently by the rest of the audience. It's a signal. With incredible unanimity, inexplicably as well, without discussing it beforehand we break into "Away in a Manger" and "Silent Night". That's really Christmassy!

The Mare

Jacques rides on horseback at the edge of the forest between the meadow and the clearing. The sun's rays, carried by the wind, stain the grass with dappled light. He raises his head and inhales the breeze in the leafy branches. He quickens his pace. The trees thin out and then disappear completely, replaced by yellow grasses which bend with his passage. His mount shakes her wild mane, releasing a fragrance which is pungent and soft at the same time. He lightly arches his back, pressing his calves against the quivering flanks. The mare rears up and bolts forward, straight into the blood-flecked wheat. He accelerates, knees clamped against the withers, reigns barely tightened, his gaze on the horizon. The ears of wheat give way to stubble fields where the reapers have already passed. He murmurs to himself :

"Ba da boom, ba da boom," imitating the sound of the hooves striking the ground. Piles of straw, lifted in his wake like bits of dust, whirl in the air before falling in his tracks. Nothing matters but this mad ride across the fields, further and further into the cool morning air. Hunched over the flowing mane, raised on his stirrups, he encourages the animal, who flicks her ears at the sound of his voice. Magnetized together by a combined force of love and of friendship, they jump a hedge without slowing the pace, soaring into the air. Obstacles no longer exist for this unique couple, rolling on the wave of their fantasy.

The sky grows dark, weighted with thick clouds carried by gusts of wind. The ground becomes marshy with madder, blackens, bursts with puddles from which jabbering and grumbling crows drink. Under the weight of the clouds, heavy with sadness, the horse loses its speed, breathing heavily. Soon the rain blinds them. Dripping wet, they plod further along in furious whirlwinds which transform the rutted road into a mire. The horse slips and sinks. Jacques pulls on the reigns, but in vain. In mud up to her knees, her nostrils steaming, foaming at the mouth, the beast whinnies, panicking, her eyes rolling in fear. Finally she frees herself. Beating her shoes, her hooves covered in blood, she falls to her chest, toppling over on her side. Bathed in sweat, Jacques struggles beneath the dangerous mass which smothers him involuntarily.

Tangled in his bedding, his legs immobile, chained to his board, he looks incomprehensively at the silver ball fastened to the wall. He slowly remembers the walls which enclose him, feels his body tighten with painful fury. One by one, the half-light reveals to him objects which are only too familiar. The table, the chair, the bookcase with its books, the sink with its white earthenware basin. Two meters from him, although everything has the same indefinite grey tint, the contours of the door are clearly distinguishable.

As always, after his dream he feels a gnawing, monotonous torpor beneath his melancholy. His limbs tensed, his groin on fire, he endures the erection which brings him back to life, rooting itself solidly in the pit of his lower abdomen. His hand, hesitant at first, reaches under the sheet. His naked penis pulses rhythmically and hopefully. Furiously, his fingers curled, he grips himself with gentle firmness, wearily repeating the undeniable, redeeming movements.

Relentlessly, the incessant up and down movement brings him closer to climax. He feels the force of the moment rising in him. Frantic, his arm moves more and more swiftly, the hollow of his palm intensifying the rubbing. A white flash of lightning passes through his swollen stiffness, exploding before his eyes, which stare into nothingness. His jaws slack, hanging open, panting, his fingers release their prey. Without thinking, he cautiously touches the viscous thread spread over his side, running drop by drop into a fold in his sweaty, rumpled bed. Without moving, he catches his breath. His head spins with sterile thoughts in the treachery of his unsated, inextinguishable desire.

Jacques snorts abruptly, driving the persistent rancor of his memory deep within him. He had thought that Christian and Claudine were his friends. It was at their house that he had taken refuge with bloodied hands. Christian had been out, and it was to Claudine that he had told his story, interrupted with sobs and hiccoughs. Claudine had called the cops. Stunned, unable to react, he had overheard his friend's treason. Christian had come back right when the officers were putting him into the van. He had accompanied him to the station. They had made the trip without a word. Christian had grasped and interpreted his silence, revealing the scale of the tragedy with a complete lack of consolation.

The perpetrator of a violent crime, they had put him in isolation. As it had been a Friday night, he had spent two whole days without any news at all. They had brought him sandwiches and coffee in a paper cup. He hadn't been allowed to wash or to shave. On the Monday morning, the lawyer sent by Christian had demanded that they allow him to shower. The examining judge had recommended incarceration. He had wanted to protest, but for what? It was a woman; she had cited the risk of a second offense. As a result, he had deduced that Jeannine had pressed charges. He had regretted not having killed her. An unrestrained hatred had darkened his vision for a moment. The judge must have noticed it, because she had recoiled slightly. On his next visit, the lawyer had told him to control his emotions from then on, to at least try to appear more contrite; if not repentant, less arrogant, to smile a little, not too much, to lower his eyes; in short to seem more inoffensive.

His temples beating with pulsing blood, like a malfunctioning automaton, his mechanical steps strike the paving stones which lead him toward his destiny. Conscious of his forbidden, ruthless cruelty, he continues, incapable of stopping the madness which forces him where he does not want to go. Vengeance drones in his ringing ears, forcing him to proceed and erasing his thoughts. He's himself and someone else. He looks at himself, observes his movements, the passion which holds him captive is stronger than he. To destroy her is all that he desires, to erase the insult, to make her pay for her treachery, to eliminate her for the awful pain he feels throbbing beneath his ribs, to make her suffer, to give her back the pain she inflicted on him. To kill her.

His fingers tightened around the handle of the knife at the bottom of his pocket, he slips through the labyrinth of streets, carried along by the dark intoxication of a hostile, destructive bitterness. He rings her bell, shouts her name. Asks to see her. Climbs the stairs. She is standing before him. Out on the landing, she looks at him with a smile on her face. Rage dictates his gestures. With force, with excess, a taste of love, of death, and of blood in his mouth, he brings down the blade.

She falls at his feet. He strikes more brutally. She curls herself up into a ball. Implacable, he continues stabbing. His fury subsided, his arms dangling at his sides, crushed by the growing sensation of an appalling mistake, through a fog he sees Jeannine stagger to her feet and reenter the apartment. Two dismayed friends approach her, uttering a few words.

"This is unbelievable," he hears her sad voice say. He has nothing more to do here. No one thinks to close the door. No one pays attention to him. Weary, he goes back down the stairs. Tears run down his cheeks.

His face buried in his pillow, Jacques cries. He hadn't been able to prevent Jeannine from reaching for the stars, toward a new love, from being happy in someone else's arms. Smothered in regret, he blows his nose, gets up, and walks to the sink. He carefully washes his face. Surly, he growls between his teeth, "Christmas, my ass!"

Little Viviane

Cosily snuggled up under the down of his duvet, Charles dozes on. Suddenly, the patter of bare feet on the parquet floor wakes him. He yawns, carefully lifting his eyelids. The familiar image of Viviane bent over him filters through the eyelashes of his half-open eyes.

"Charles! Charles!"

"Hmm…"

"Come on! Quick! Get up!"

"Shhhh!!"

"I heard them!"

Her little hand starts tugging at him energetically. Good little prince, Charles sits up, runs his fingers through his thick hair, and, throwing his covers completely to the side, sits on the edge of the bed. Viviane indulges him with a radiant smile, illuminating her dimples. Patiently, knowing herself to be irresistible, she waits for his full attention.

"He shouted, 'Ho! Ho! Ho!' I was listening. Their hooves made noise on the roof tiles."

"Well, we'll have to go check it out."

"Yes! Yes! They've come for sure."

Carried away with joy, Viviane claps her hands and throws her head back in laughter.

In a sky-blue nightgown, her head tilted back, curls spread over her slightly rounded forehead, she is like a cherub which watches you from the corner of its eye. Three years her senior, Charles feels responsible for his sister. She's so innocent. How naïve to believe in Santa Claus! To disillusion her, however, is the last thing he wants to do. He lets himself be won over by the contagious enthusiasm of the little magician, who with one pirouette can transport him back to the land of the fairies.

"Calm down. You're going to wake the whole house."

She knows that her brother needs a little time to wake up and that afterward he will do everything she desires. Tirelessly, he'll play her games, take her on walks, teach her a thousand things. She and Charles adore one another; they're inseparable. However today she regrets her brother's slowness. She's so impatient to discover her presents. They haven't talked about anything else for days.

Last week, Grandpa went with her to visit Santa Claus. They went down to the train station and took the train, which they rarely do, but Grandpa hates driving in the city. He abhors the traffic jams and the underground parking lots. Once when he had taken Grandma to do some shopping in the big department stores, he lost the car in the maze of levels. He hadn't understood what the numbers and letters were for. As for Grandma, she has a profound dislike for concrete basements from which you can only exit via an elevator and enter through a tunnel. "It's too distressing," she would say.

Viviane adored this word. She would impersonate Grandma, imitating her way of taking in a sharp little breath before speaking and enunciating each syllable: DIS-TRESS-

ING. She would make her voice a little hoarse when she did it.

In the train, Grandpa had explained to her that she should always stay with him because there would probably be a big crowd as Santa Claus was very popular and many children just like her would be coming to see him. Excited by the idea of meeting the old man, she had asked Grandpa dozens of questions, which he had answered in detail, painting her an accurate picture.

She had recognized him as soon as she saw him. The lights, the noises, the shouts, the music; everything had disappeared. There was nothing left but Him. The multitude of gifts which surrounded her vanished in His presence. He reigned over a crowd of little heads on a chair gleaming with gold and precious stones, mounted on a platform enclosed by pine trees decorated with a thousand lights. Her eager eyes devoured him; she didn't dare breathe. Grandpa had put her letter into her hands and, after putting her down, had gently pushed her through the throngs of respectful children. She had timidly awaited her turn, carefully mounting the steps one by one. Standing near him, her moistened lips half-open in rapture, she marveled at him, dazzled by the scarlet accentuated with white. He had bent towards her, murmuring words she no longer heard, and had put his hands on her waist. He had then lifted her onto his knee. Terrified and thrilled at the same time, she had sought the eyes of Grandpa, at first without success but finding his face half-hidden by a pine branch before she was seized by panic. Thus reassured, she had handed her missive to

Santa Claus, who took it in his gloved hand. Emboldened, she had assured him that she had been good all year, omitting a few unimportant details, and she had invited him to come to her house. Smiling, he accepted. A camera lunged from the crowd, blinding them with its flash. Carried through the air, she found herself back in Grandpa's arms.

She had no memory of going home, if only because she had saved this marvelous vision behind her closed eyelids, faking sleep in order to prolong the dream-like vision. The next few days had been agony; she couldn't do anything but wait. Finally the day had come.

Charles stands up, taking her by the hand. Without a word, they head for the staircase. Silently, holding her breath with immense expectation, she reaches the bottom of the stairs. The doors to the living room are wide open. Her feet planted solidly in the softness of the carpet, transfixed with stupefaction, she is unable to move. Towering where yesterday there was only the bay window is a giant blue spruce.

The silver tuft at the top reaches the ceiling, the snow-laden branches stretch to the corners, and glass spheres, frosted pinecones, and golden balls hang among the skillfully arranged garlands. A bunny beats a drum slung across its shoulder with miniature drumsticks, reflective birds cling to the needles, chirping and bobbing their flickering tails. The bells of the carousel horses jingle as they go up and down and a speeding skier slaloms to the tip of a branch. Above the manger tucked between the rocks at the foot of the tree, a star slightly twinkles. Every lock of the angel's hair matches its multicolored radiance.

"He kept his promise! He came!" murmurs Viviane, standing astounded before the ribbon-trimmed packages scattered over the carpet. Every shape and color is represented in the joyous blend of bows, knots, and wrapping paper. A surge of emotion floods her heart, and as it passes through her removes any trace of self-control. She stamps her feet with joy.

"Christmas! Christmas! It's Christmas! Daddy! Mommy! Grandpa! Grandma! It's Christmas!" shouts Viviane, running joyfully into the refuge of Grandpa's arms.

Christmas Eve

Surrounded by the beam of the streetlight, shoes march past cautiously, level with the basement window. The molten snow and black ice have signaled the precariousness of the ground, which leads them to walk in an affected way, with an unconfessed reserve. Some, big and clunky, come down without any visible hesitation, while others, those of fancy shoes, show a barely perceptible trial and error; testing the ground before they trust themselves to it. Sylvia watches the comings and goings on the sidewalk for hours, looking for a small pair among the multitudes. The moment they pass before the window, they belong to her. She loves colorful pumps but they're getting rarer and rarer. Chunky, wide heels are in fashion, preferably black. This is her way of going window-shopping. Protected by the windows, she likes to imagine the bodies above the calves. Sometimes two pairs walk at the same pace; then she sees two people intertwined, murmuring pledges of love. But today they all seem to be in a hurry, despite the dubious quality of the sidewalk. They hasten along toward their destination in the cold, toward the warmth of a family and the comfort of a home.

Since Dupont died, Sylvia is alone. Together they would go for long walks along the Seine, just for the healthy pleasure of walking. Summer and winter the quays offered sights which were both admirable and free of charge. Despite his old age, Dupont remained alert to the details of the street, sniffed at every tuft of grass, succeeded in hunting stray butterflies along the edge of the water. He never needed coaxing to go out. Remembering, a deep sigh escapes her and she absentmindedly draws her anorak around her shoulders. Dupont had hated having to move continually.

She pulls herself together. She shouldn't complain. Procrastination is useless, even dangerous. There were people much worse off than she. Of course, it had been hard losing Dupont, but she would certainly find an abandoned puppy in a garbage can come spring. She saw them every year. Besides, hadn't she had the good luck to discover this abandoned cellar for the winter, while many others would have to make do with cardboard boxes, at the mercy of bad weather and garbage men?

Satisfied, she stops watching the street theater to inspect her newly acquired estate. The surrounding darkness in contrast with the brightness from outside makes her blink her eyes several times. She systematically appraises each of her proudly owned possessions. She considers each crate, each plank, piled against the wall where she organizes her retrieved newspapers and magazines. Appreciating her collection, she observes that she has built up a nice little library. What does it matter if the armchair's springs have punctured its threadbare jute cover or if the lack of light deprives her of the pleasure of reading! With the corner furnished like that, it brings to mind the cozy look of a home. She gazes tenderly at the ruined mattress against the opposite wall.

She had discovered it one morning a few streets away and had hastened to drag it back to her lair. The cover had suffered a little from the journey but nonetheless appeared quite acceptable, without any noticeable holes. Using wire racks as a box spring, she lay it in a corner sheltered from drafts. Every night since, stretched out on the softness of her bed, she thanked her star for watching over her, congratulating herself for having had the strength to drag it all the way here. Thanks to the covers piled onto the pallet, she can take part in the ritual of going to bed and getting up every day, taking off her clothes in the evening and putting them back on in the morning, without fear of catching her death of cold.

The fantasy of having a well-organized life helps her to survive. Whatever the weather, in every season, she leaves early to make her rounds. Precise and efficient, she meticulously inspects the piles of garbage, filling her shopping bag with every useful thing she finds, as well as appetizing leftovers which she takes for lunch in the square. Even if it rains she rarely returns here, rather taking shelter under a porch in a quiet little street. She has her habits, but takes care to change her routine daily for fear she is being watched.

Often when the weather is nice she goes up to Sacré-Cœur, not to enjoy the view of Paris but because the people there are more generous than at Notre-Dame. She extends her hand, seated at the foot of the steps. Most of the visitors give her a coin or a bill, especially foreigners. They don't dare refuse her solicitation. Her needy appearance, her fresh breath, her smoothly tied-back hair, and her politely outstretched hand encourage them to give. She suspects them of being ashamed of the sophisticated gear slung over their shoulders before her obvious poverty. Their uncertainty does not even come close to her daily reality.

The day before yesterday she went to the Père Lachaise cemetery by way of the rue Turbigo. Initially she had intended to go to the kitchens at the Hôpital Saint-Louis, but without really realizing it she had taken a right, entering the avenue de la République. Liberty! Equality! Fraternity! - three words which left her feeling doubtful.

The main entrance to the cemetery, on the boulevard de Ménilmontant, with at the end of the grand avenue the colossal monument to the dead, inspired her to go for a stroll. She visited Colette after Mademoiselle Lenormand, then Rossini and Alfred de Musset. Preoccupied by her game, she turned off to the left at the top of the stairs, heading toward Bizet and Enesco. More steps and then Raymond Radiguet stood greeting her. On the other side, near the Grand Nord crossroads, Grétry, Méhul, Pleyel, Chopin, Cherubini and Bellini awoke snatches of memories of former lives in her. She stretched out on a stone and would have wanted to stay there, lying on the white marble, surrounded by accents which had once soothed her, but the biting cold had forced her to leave. She had picked a boxwood branch growing next to a cross. Returning by way of the boulevard de

Magenta, she was on time for the seven-thirty mass.

Her plunder protected under her coat, she had wandered through the maze of little streets. While walking past the Galeries Lafayette, she had been struck by the number of lights. A chestnut vendor presented her with the gift of a cone of roasted chestnuts, which she had enjoyed while admiring the illuminated garlands. At that moment, she had decided to decorate her abode.

Sylvia blocks the windows against drafts with boards, stopping up the cracks with rags. She takes a box of matches out of her pocket and makes her way toward the stub of candle which she can find in the dark. The room fills with a soft glow, revealing walls stained with streaks of saltpeter which drip relentlessly into stagnant pools in the street-side corner.

In the ceiling, black liquid oozes from a straw-stuffed crack along a pipe coated in plaster. She sees none of this; her treasures are displayed on the squared-off planks which serve as a stand. Filled with wonder, Sylvia examines them with the gleeful eye of ownership. To anyone else, they would be a mass of garbage good only for throwing away, but to her they are cherished things; they share a common history. She remembers that the glass pot in which the boxwood branch stands came from the Gare du Nord, out of a garbage can on a Thalys coming from Belgium. It had been almost full when she had reached in to root it out of the bin. The porcelain plate was a present from the rue Mouffetard, one rainy night. The cup, the mug, the carafe; all speak a language only she can decipher, saying words only she hears.

But tonight she hardly listens to her old friends. What stirs her the most, demands all her attention, is the little tree she has made from discarded branches planted in a bucket of sand. She has hung candy wrappers and bits of plastic bag among the needles, and twirled aluminum foil around the bark. The masterpiece of all the ornaments is a Santa Claus, survivor of the gutter on the rue Monsieur le Prince.

On a mangled chair, her loaded shopping bag assures her of an extraordinary feast. Tonight she's eating in; it's Christmas Eve. She rummages in a pile of rags at the foot of the bed, extracting a large red cloth. She unfolds it carefully, shakes it forcefully, and makes of it an amaranth tablecloth which she lavishly spreads out. The folds fall to the ground, emanating an antiquated feel. From a bag, she takes out a whole loaf of bread and a tin of cassoulet with a gaudy label. For dessert there is a caramel flan in a pale plastic container.

She sits on the wobbly stool, wedges the cassoulet in the crook of her elbow, and pulls the aluminum tab. The lid lifts, curls, and detaches with ease. She lifts the white beans to her nose, breathes in deeply, smells the cooked aroma with exquisite delight, plunges her fork into the congealed mass, vigilantly inspects the ingredients, and fishes out the microscopic bits of bacon and sausage, which she lines up on the edge of her plate, saving them for last. With the help of a spoon, she scrapes the bottom of the tin, salvaging every last bit of aspic. Ready to revel in the meal, she carefully examines the heap of gelatin before her.

There is an inquisitive rustling near the door. Her heart skips a beat, full of fear. The impossible has occurred. Dupont is there, behind the wood. She opens her eyes so wide they hurt, trying to drive the darkness away. Her chest freezes; she stops breathing. Nothing. She must have imagined it. Suddenly sad despite the feast spread out before her, she is astonished by the hope which carried her beyond death, bowling her over at the slightest thing, cornering her in her crazy thoughts. Again there is a persistent little scratch. She slowly turns her head, squinting at the dark in every nook and cranny. Atop a beam, in the absolute impenetrableness of night, two glowing red points brazenly look her up and down, staring at her with their impudent incandescence. Comforted, she begins to eat. A sense of well-being sweeps over her in large, incessant waves, restoring her with a beneficial warmth. She feels like laughing and like crying. She won't be alone tonight.

E la nave va

Her gaze lost in the wake's milky trail
marbled with lapis lazuli, jade and sapphire,
the silhouette watches the cheerful porpoises
leap from the foam to greet her. Her thoughts
drift, framed by the orange and lemon trees
caressing the forged iron arabesques of their
glossy leaves, sheltering fruit which promises
sweet future delights.

Tireless crickets pierce the night, calling
forcefully back and forth from one wall to the
other. At times they abruptly cease their
racket for no apparent reason, the silence

making way for the commotion which they begin all the more all the more vigorously a few moments later. Their ardor is only equaled by that of the cicadas who take over from them at the faintest glimmer of dawn, which polishes the emerald of the languid sea in the cove of the bay with mother of pearl and mottled silver, where pebbles, worn from their wild escapades, end up cradled by molten malachite. At the foot of the rounded church lie the ancestors' funereal stones, the final resting place for the country's children. The marble walls throw back the light that strikes them, milky mirrors of rock crystal where nothing is reflected and where everyone find themselves.

A few rounded tile roofs are hidden in the greenery like ripe oranges in giant trees. Devilish cacti line the winding paths and the electricity poles are plugged with immense palms. Others, with leafy branches, disappear from the road's edge, gathering ecstatically in the bright ditches in which unreliable streams shamelessly drench the parched ground. Fig trees, their fingers spread wide, show the way, charitably offering their full purses to the passers-by.

In the air, ecstatic swallows hunt, twirling up to the zenith, gulping dragonflies in the meanderings of the warm breezes. Flowering bougainvilleas attack the roofs, competing energetically with the indigo clematis and the gleaming honeysuckle, spreading their fragrances softened in the nascent heat.

After a few days of fury caused by a combination of the full moon and an earthquake, the sea has calmed a bit. Solitary foaming waves pound the stones weighed down by millennia of rolling, recalling the past turbulence with their victorious plumes. Pale showers crash against the shore, splattering with rainbows and sea spray the bathers aligned in offering to the sun on their multicolored beds. For a moment, a roiling foam blocks the pebbles, kicked up shamelessly by the suddenly turbulent water, from inquisitive glances. Everything merges into a playful whirlpool. Languorous hisses are followed by the high-pitched rasping of stones dragged pitilessly by the merciless undertow which carelessly swallows the plaintive struggle of the waves crushed by its powerful blast. The undulations repeat endlessly, although certain modulations can be perceived by a watchful eye or attentive ear. Fishermen's boats buoy at the end of their tethers, are briefly concealed by a breaking wave and then triumphantly reappear at the crest of a stealthy summit, shouting into the furious wind.

Walking along the coast, she feels the power of the sea turned to steel, mercury, and silver, revealing its latent violence and force in these precursory signs of possible ravages.

They cut the engines. Dimitri has thrown the anchor. The smothered pop of a champagne cork leaves him indifferent. She slides into the blue transparence. Curious fish zigzag briskly around her, come to explore her, kiss her toes with their polished nails. Slender little submarines, decorated with colors alternately bright and soft, they come together merrily in spirited ballets of purity and exuberant energy. They lazily twirl around and then suddenly disappear in fright, striating the wave with their golden streaks.

Their fear quelled, they return to surround the calves of the swimmers, boastfully daring to make risky dives. Maria happily spots them; they are free. With a few vigorous strokes she rises toward the reflective surface, grabs the ladder, puts her foot on the bottom rung, climbs up, and takes the towel tied thoughtfully to the rail.

Refreshed, she lies in the sun although she knows that it will be harmful to her voice, as is the idleness to which she has devoted herself remorselessly for several months.

She feels his shadow on her skin before he covers her with his warmth. Her hand caresses his neck and slides to his shoulder; her foot rubs his ankle. His slowly moving fingers stir her anticipation. Sliding the thin straps from her shoulders one by one, he strips her to the waist. His lips stray from her lips to her ear. He whispers her name, nibbles at her gently, impatiently. His caresses become more directed, his mouth breathes in the scent of her breasts, his expert hands quicken, tearing the bathing suit, and then they are once again tender, causing alternating waves of pain and of delight; subtle at first, forceful at the end. Groundswells submerge her, carrying her away with their trembling rush. His silky tongue delicately explores her intimacy. Set ablaze, suffocated by her passion, she pulls him forcefully toward the depths of her thighs, arched in pleasure. To feel him inside her makes her explode with delight. Their limbs entangled, they succumb to the same passion, rolling them in wild swells of pleasure. Overcome with love, they mournfully emerge from the limbo of their intoxication. Satisfied, she curls up in the cocoon of his arms.

With Dimitri, she is a woman before all else. She hardly ever practices her scales anymore. The days stretch out lazily, without provoking her to do her singing exercises. But this morning she had sung because Dimitri had counted on her to entertain his guests. Instead of putting on the usual fireworks display, he had organized a large mass in the village of Loggos where she had played the roll of priestess. Despite the inappropriateness of his request, she had agreed to it with only one condition: that the two of them spend Christmas day alone at sea, far from everything. E la nave va.

Merry Christmas

His eyelids flutter briefly in the piercing brightness. At the same instant, a jagged graph bleeps onto the lighted glass screen. A body bends over the bloodless face. Competent, precise, clean hands bustle about. A trolley covered with an unembroidered, unembellished cloth displays instruments of torture in glinting steel. A syringe pierces a pale vein. A dismal moan, barely audible, escapes cracked, whitened lips. Joël struggles with all his might to reach the light, to escape the night.

He fights the nausea which attacks him with every sip of water, raises his abdomen in suffocating spasms with every pill. He refuses to give in to the violent, unyielding, invincible pain which wracks his insides. He curbs his suffering with more and more difficulty; his stomach contracts, retching more violently, forcing him to hyperventilate. The infernally bitter taste of tablets burns his tongue, takes hold of his senses - his sense of smell, disgusting him, attacking him. His teeth screech together, the sound bursts in his melting brain. Chattering, he bites out baffling nonsense in a jumble of muttering bogged down with saliva and restricted breath. His fingers tense around the glass of water and he drinks it in one swallow. The liquid sickens him, setting off a series of heaves and bringing tears to his eyes. A repulsive viscosity fills his half-closed mouth, spews forth, humiliating, degrading. Demeaned, he loses consciousness surrounded by his filth.

A gentle hand touches him. Whispers reach him in his cloudy limbo. A foggy glow filters shadows through his eyelashes.

Every night he sees the same outlines, wedged into their overcoats on the sidewalks lit up for the holidays. The same chalky faces, unsmiling, unspeaking, unseeing. He passes them every day along his solitary walks. Not even a hello. He tries. With a pleasant air, he approaches them, greets them. They stare at him frantically and shrink away. Frightened, they run off. That a stranger should talk to them is perplexing! Sometimes, he shouts in the middle of the street. Annoyed, they look away, preferring not to see him, or at least pretend. He knows them. He likes them. That's who they are. Dwelling in the twists and turns of shameful regrets and corrupt desires, they don't want to have anything to do with him. He watches them. Watch each other. Where is the difference? He doesn't understand. Their neat clothes. Freshly shaven. Well-groomed. They avoid his outstretched hand.

A palm rests on his forehead. Pushes back the sticky locks. The touch of cool fingers brings him relief. He bats his eyelashes, shakes his head, drives back the shock, the moment of truth. They speak to him, offer him a drink.

He can't drink. He has never liked the false friendliness of bars, the alcohol weaving an impression of conviviality around the locals which disappears as soon as they hit the street.

He never goes to bars, the noisy laughter, the loud music, the affable or abject boys, the bawdy jokes, the smoke, the gambling. The rituals of the aperitif and the white wine are as strange to him as the jeers at the market, which he rarely visits. These people who shout coarse things over the rows of stalls frighten him. He's overcome by panic at the idea that one of these words could miss its target and fall on his head. There are yellow ones which whistle cheerfully, red which buzz, black which rumble, green which bounce off the posts, smashing into the tables, and sometimes there are white which flutter about on a breath, but he's partial to the blue ones which spiral through the air, drawing scrolls in the brisk morning air. Nowhere else do words wreak such havoc.

They lift his head, fluff his pillows. He would like to plunge back into sleep so that they would leave him alone. Someone presses an object into his hands, he presses the buttons on the case.

Hundreds of people move through the mud created by the melting snow, mostly women and children. Sagging under shapeless burdens, they progress heavily in the silence, step by step, in one long, endless line. Wading through the slush, they walk along the dark road, hurrying toward a mess more deplorable than the one they just left. Hanging over the column of refugees, peace officers sheltered in tanks survey them, pointing the tips of their rifles in their direction. From the virgin summit of the hill next to them, a winged monster suddenly appears, spitting flashes of fire. The rattle of its flight rings out in a horrifying staccato through the valley. Bodies fall. Cries, sobs, and prayers raise toward the steel dragon. Deaf to their lamentations, it roars off toward the horizon. Machine gunners spring into action, united by their menace and their bullets, the individuals dispersed. The line begins walking again, taking its dead and wounded with it. On the snow, drunken stars bear witness to their passage.

Joël hides his face in the crook of his arm. Exhausted, revolted, rent with convulsions, he fidgets nervously. Someone bends back his elbow. Defeated, he opens his eyes. An angel dressed in white smiles at him.

"Merry Christmas."

"Merry Christmas," he replies automatically.

Very very quietly, he cries like a small child.

The First Day of Christmas

Incredulous, I catch sight of the pallid plates. In their centers, peeled tomatoes insolently flaunt themselves. Intrigued, I see only them, blatant presumptions circled in gold on the opaline porcelain. I shake hands mechanically, the names flit around me without registering with the friendly faces. My first contact with my husband's family, reunited in its entirety around a table decorated at each end by a miniature plant with dark brick-colored star-shaped leaves, coincides with Christmas dinner. We are not in the least late, and yet all faces turn to us when we arrive, seeming offended beneath the displayed smiles, full of an unspoken reproach. Apparently we should have come earlier to drink the inevitable cup of coffee which in the Netherlands takes the place of an aperitif, but we had wanted to skip that trying preliminary! My mother-in-law urges me to take my seat, between a large woman with thick blond hair spilling over her shoulders and my father-in-law, who governs. My husband sits facing me, to the right of his father. One of the daughters helps the mother, carrying in several silver platters, the covers of which hide their contents from me.

Through the glass doors of the living room, the lighted tree announces that it is a holiday, but tomorrow will be as well as there are two days of Christmas, the first reserved for the family, the second for friends. On the other hand they have no tradition of Christmas Eve, not commemorating either the birth of Christ or the Advent of Saint Sylvester.

Serving drinks is Chris's responsibility. Being married to a Frenchwoman, it is his duty to be the expert. That he is serving a Riesling only adds to the prestige surrounding him! I can't take my eyes off of the fragile nudity of the tomatoes. Everyone spouts their knowledge on the different wines of France. Out of politeness with regards to me, the discussion of their respective qualities takes place in French. I love it when the Dutch speak my language. Deliberately, scrupulously seeking their words, using their innate sense of language, they construct semantically correct sentences, the syntactic precision of which delights me. What they say is completely without importance, but their manner of expressing it, with the cheerful coherence of a technician, receives my complete admiration.

Horrified, I watch my father-in-law grab the sugar bowl and sprinkle it generously over his tomato, imitated by the other guests. In desperation, my eyes seek the salt shakers which have not yet made their appearance among the silver, porcelain, and crystal. In great distress I realize the treachery of my husband, usually keen on French dishes, who follows the example of his parents, mincing the fruit of the Aztecs and eating it with a small spoon as if it were a succulent dessert. No one pays attention to my plate and I munch on the fruit without seasoning, cursing the vinaigrette-ignorant fools. The household help is absent and the youngest sister provides the service, changing the place settings, collecting the red-streaked porcelain.

"In your honor, we're eating our dinner in the French style. That's why we had an appetizer before the soup."

I sit astounded, speechless. From a pale, bland liquid without any pronounced flavor I deduce a Dutch-style asparagus consommé, presented luxuriously in silver soup plates.

Directly from the kitchen, served from one large platter, is carried a slice of roast pork accompanied by sautéed potatoes, Brussels sprouts, and applesauce. I listen with pleasure to my family-in-law discuss the recipes. The Dutch are gourmands in their own way, although personally I find that the consistency of their dishes balances generally between that of baby applesauce and canned dog food.

My opinion is yet again reinforced at this dinner where the guests shamelessly mash their vegetables with their forks and carefully mix them with the potatoes, which have been crushed into a puree, and with their meat, which they have cut into tiny pieces. They turn everything into a thick, smooth paste, drench it copiously with the fatty jus which overflows the gravy boats, and crown the top with a pile of crudités in mayonnaise.

My father-in-law, a university professor emeritus, keeps the conversation on the culinary arts, divided by his concern not to disgust me entirely and his personal preference. He has obviously made a break in his habitual manner of eating. His meat has remained intact alongside the mashed Brussels sprouts and sautéed potatoes. He launches into a detailed description of the unusual dishes he has been invited to eat during his numerous travels. Saharan charcoal-grilled snake, Malaysian monkey-eye soup, poached goat testicles in the Gobi Desert, Tanzanian grilled grasshoppers; he could go on forever. Chewing absent-mindedly, I listen politely. His French is perfect, his elocution elegant, his choice of words precise. He tells his stories with amusing loquaciousness, mingling his personal point of view with indisputable facts. He concocts witty stories, charming his audience. He had submitted to all local customs so as not to offend his hosts. Through the enchantment of his words, the morale appears, only just scarcely disguised. I want to as well but my tastebuds revolt at the hodgepodge on the plates.

I gather my thoughts. The red cabbage, cooked into a shapeless, colorless muck and soured by the inevitable dash of vinegar, accompanied by blood sausage cut into slices as thick as mortadella, finely chopped escarole mixed with mashed potatoes, sauerkraut mashed with boiled potatoes, and the margarine which replaces butter on square toasts of soft white bread without crusts, all make up a spectacular exoticism within his reach but invisible from his point of view. Just like this meal which ends abruptly, without cheese or dessert, on a virginal, unsullied tablecloth, without an orgiastic trace, lifeless.

X Mas

The noises from the street bounce around her without reaching her. She hears only the quiet purr of the limousine. The smoked-glass windows protect her from curious glances without isolating her. At the airport, the employees called to one another joyously. Every traveler was granted the customary "Merry Christmas" in addition to the official stamp on their passport. At the exit from customs, the giant tree told her it was Christmas. The familiar spectacle of passing strangers diverted her impatience. Another few minutes and she would be in Manhattan.

The snow had invaded the park where the bare trunks carry one's eyes far over the landscape. The Hudson gives off its light, patiently stretching along the river carved in the ice. At this early hour, its banks clear of any trace accommodate wintry skeletons only. Many-colored jays flit about in the branches, staining the white blanket heaped at their feet with azure and rust.

He lights the candles, moves a candelabra, pauses near the coffeepot. In two or three minutes, she'll be there.

They cross Brooklyn Bridge. The chauffeur steers the heavy vehicle through traffic with dexterity. He knows his odd habit of always going by way of City Hall, Bleecker Street, Greenwich, and Chelsea to reach the West Side. He respects his way of reinstating contact with the city, of silently savoring his return, the reunions. In the past, she had liked going via Broadway, Fifth Avenue, and crossing the Park, but they had started taking a different route to avoid bad memories since the incident.

She can't keep herself from staring at the bushes along the side of the road, however invisible. Dread pushes her deeply into the leather cushions, locks her into a somber deafness. The beating of her heart makes her short of breath. Prostrate with the pounding blood which reddens her ears, her nostrils dilated, she submits to the hand which forces her to relax her clenched jaws, to the other which tears at her sweater while a merciless knee pins down her thighs. Powerless, she sniffs back mucus mixed with tears of spite, rage, and terror. She screams at the hand which stifles her, she shrieks at the fist which hammers her temples, she shouts at the fingernails which dig at her breasts. The impact of the filthy insults hurts more than the blows. The hot sticky liquid coats her throat and lips. Revolted by fear and shame, she exits the thicket, her arms wedged against her body.

Instinctively, she draws her cape around her. The snow on the sidewalks remains intact.

In an apartment on Riverside Drive, a giant Christmas tree stands on the point of collapsing under its decorations. The potent green riddled with red and blue sparkles beneath garlands of gold and of silver. Multicolored lights blink intermittently, in tandem with many large white stars. At its base, a snowman keeps watch over a pile of parcels wrapped in brightly shining paper.

Some display carefully ironed bows, others with curls as big as cabbages, matching their ribbons. Bright stripes speckled with glitter wrap around the smallest ones.

He inspects the mountain of gifts one last time. Eager to celebrate her return, their friends had all brought welcome-home presents. She's coming back from a long journey. He waits for her.

Crouching in the muddy delta of her nightmarish memories, her thoughts swelled by the torture of her caustic memory, revolted, she shivers in the cocoon-like warmth. The silence is without appeal, without hope. It will never be Christmas again.

Murielle Lucie Clément

Imprimé par CreateSpace
Dépôt légal octobre 2015